BILL and the MAZE
at
GRIMLEY GRANGE

Anthony Stones

WOLFHOUND PRESS

For Camilla

J92,254.

© 1990 Anthony Stones

Published 1990 by
WOLFHOUND PRESS
68 Mountjoy Square,
Dublin 1.

£4.99.

British Library Cataloguing in Publication Data

Stones, Anthony
  Bill and the maze at Grimley Grange.
  I. Title
  823'.914[J]

  ISBN 0-86327-249-5

Wolfhound Press receives financial assistance from the Arts Council (An Chomhairle Ealaíon) Dublin, Ireland.

Cover design and illustration: Anthony Stones
Typesetting: Redsetter Ltd., Dublin.
Printed and bound by Proost.

Bill Williams had a plan — to beat the Maze at Grimley Grange.

From his bedroom window he could see it in the moonlight.

It looked easy . . .

He would find
his way to the
middle and out again
before Grandad peeped in on the way to bed.

'Well — here goes,' thought Bill.

Ooops! – He had almost forgotten his ball of string.
He would need it to find his way out of the maze.

He tip-toed past Grandad's room . . .

down the stairs . . .

out of the Grange, and round the front . . .

He strode past the topiary . . .

to the entrance of the MAZE.

He tied his string to the bottom of the first shrub.

Then he set off inside, letting out the string in a trail behind him. At first . . . he did quite well.

But when he came to a dead end, he had to turn around and go back on his tracks.

Just around a corner, he heard a snuffling and a grunting . . . WAS IT A MONSTER?

But it was only a hedgehog on its nightly prowl!
When it saw Bill, it was more scared than he was
and quickly rolled itself up into

. . . a BALL.

Bill stared for ages at the
spikey bundle. But when it
didn't move, he crept carefully
around it and pressed on.

This way seemed better.

But then, if he turned around, so did the other!
And the other . . . and the other . . .

'I must make up my mind!' thought Bill.

He decided on the first way and, to his relief, came to an opening.

Lucky for Bill, he chose the one that led him almost to the middle of the maze.

Bill began to tread carefully . . .

He didn't REALLY believe in monsters . . . but just in case there was one, it would pay to be cautious. He put down each foot very gingerly.

He didn't notice something on the ground and when he trod on it, there was . . .

an almighty SCREECH!!

Bill nearly jumped
out of his skin.
But it wasn't a monster.
It was the CAT!

It grabbed Bill's reel of string
and dashed away . . .

Without the string how could he find his way out?
Bill was STUCK. What a CAT-astrophe!

Meanwhile, the Ghost of Grimley Grange had stepped out of his picture frame to make his nightly walk of the tower.

Now, as you know, the Ghost of Grimley Grange hated cats. In fact, he was VERY scared of them.

When he heard the cat screech, he jumped even more than Bill had done.

13

He peeped over the battlements . . . and he saw the cat racing out of the maze with the string trailing from its mouth. But something else near the middle of the maze caught his eye . . .

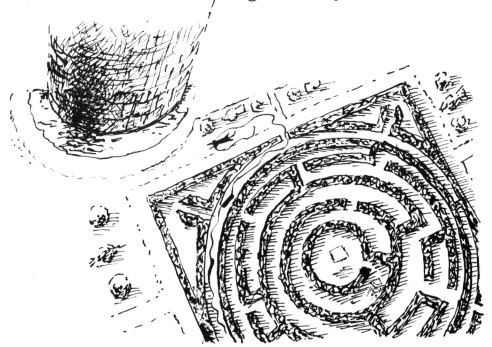

It was Bill's new paper helmet shining in the moonlight.

'But look here,' the Ghost said to himself. 'That boy was brave enough to help you once. Don't be such a COWARD. Go down this minute and help him out of the maze.'

Meanwhile Bill was trying to get out of the maze. He walked and walked and walked . . . but he kept coming to dead ends.

He tried looking under the hedges but they were too thick.

He even tried climbing to the top of the hedges but they just bent right over. Then, a cloud went over the moon . . .

A flash of lightning crossed the sky

. . . followed by a roll of thunder.

'Oh dear! Now it's going to rain as well.
I'd better hurry up,' Bill said to himself.

Suddenly, a voice said 'Hello'. 'Up here,' called
the voice.

Bill looked up and there, to his surprise, was . . .

his friend, the Ghost of Grimley Grange.

'Grammercy!' exclaimed Bill.

'That's nice,' smiled the Ghost. 'You've remembered my word.'

'How did you know I was here?' asked Bill.

'Oh, we ghosts find out what's going on,' the Ghost answered.

'But how did you know
the way?' asked Bill,
'It's so complicated.'
'Easy,' said the Ghost,

'You see, I planted the maze in the first place.
Mind you, that was *hundreds* of years ago and I'm
a bit rusty. But if I get stuck, I can do this!'

And just then . . .

another flash of lightning made them both jump.

'Grammercy! That gave me a fright,' cried the Ghost.

'And now it's going to rain,' said Bill.

'That's alright,' said the Ghost. 'Rain just goes right through ghosts. But, oh dear, you're going to be soaked.'

Bill wished he had brought his raincoat.

'Hey! I've just remembered something,' said the Ghost suddenly. 'Come over here.'

They went through the gap – and YES! . . .

They were standing right in the MIDDLE of the maze. There was a slab of stone on the ground. 'Give me a hand to push it,' said the Ghost.

They both pushed very hard and the stone began to slide away, revealing . . .

a hole and steps leading down under the GROUND.

'I'd forgotten all about this,' said the Ghost. 'It was my secret passage for getting out of the castle if my enemies ever won.'

'WOW!' said Bill.

'And now let's get you out of this rain,' said the Ghost. To Bill's relief, knowing what a coward the Ghost really was, the GHOST went first.

At the bottom of the steps was the entrance to a
cobwebby tunnel.

The Ghost just glided through the cobwebs but Bill
had to cut them with his sword.

'The Tube!' announced Bill. 'It's just like the Tube.'

It was easy for Bill to see inside the tunnel because
the Ghost lit it up.

They passed other tunnels which led off the one they were following and it seemed to Bill there was something familiar about it all.

'Aren't we going in circles?' he asked the Ghost.

'I always knew you were a bright lad,' replied the Ghost. 'What do you think is happening?'

'Well,' said Bill thoughtfully . . . 'I think it's another MAZE!'

'Right first time,' said the Ghost. 'My word, you ARE a clever lad. I did it on purpose to confuse my enemies and slow them down if they chased me out of the castle.'

'But what about the one upstairs?' asked Bill.

'Same thing,' said the Ghost. 'You can't be too careful.'

They went on for a while and Bill was thinking
about what the Ghost had said.
'But' — began Bill . . .

'But what?' asked the Ghost.
'But they caught up with you eventually – your
enemies?' said Bill.

'Oh you mean this?'
asked the Ghost,
pointing to where
his head used to be.

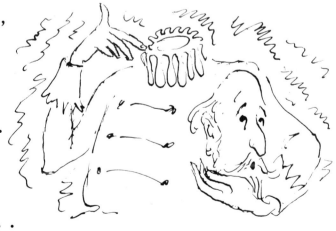

'I'd rather not talk
about *that*. It's a . . .

VERY painful subject.'
'Sorry,' said Bill. 'I didn't mean to upset you.'
'Mind you, if I'd had brave chaps like you with
me it might never have happened,' said the Ghost.
'My lot all ran away.'
'I wouldn't have,' said Bill.

'I'm sure you wouldn't,' said the Ghost.

They went round one more corner and up some steps . . . and the Ghost said: 'Well, here we are.' But all Bill could see was a blank wall.

'Watch this,' said the Ghost. He pressed his finger on a carved flower . . . and the wall opened.

'FAN-TAS-TIC!' said Bill.

'Quite so,' said the Ghost. When they stepped through, Bill got an even bigger surprise.

They were INSIDE Grimley Grange. And there, on the other side of the wall, was the Ghost's picture.

'SURPRISED?' smiled the Ghost.

'WOW!' said Bill. 'That's A-MAZING!'

'And now, after a crack like that,' said the Ghost, 'it's straight to bed for you. Come on!'

They had to be careful going past Grandad's room.

But there he was, still watching TV.

Bill was very glad to be tucked up in his bed again.
'Thanks Ghost,' said Bill.
'That's alright,' said the Ghost, 'One good turn
deserves another, I always say,' and off he floated

through the door, back to his picture.

The next morning at breakfast time
Grandad said, 'I could have sworn
I put my ball of string just here.
I wonder where it's got to?'

Bill swallowed hard.
'Well you see Grandad,'
he began, 'It was like this . . .'